Victoria 1000 X 5

Children's Book Recycling Project

Did you know? Creating the habit of nightly bedtime reading "adds up" to this: By the time your child enters school, he or she will hear stories from 1000 books or more! Read to your child each day and begin literacy development, a stronger connection to you, and a lifetime love of books.

Please accept this gift of a book as a reminder of the importance of reading to young children and help support our goal—that all children in Victoria will have at least a thousand books read to them before they enter Kindergarten.

The ***Victoria "1000 X 5" Children's Book Recycling Project*** is a partnership between Greater Victoria School District #61.
Thanks to Telus, Rotary, Island Savings, Bosa Properties, Santas Anonymous

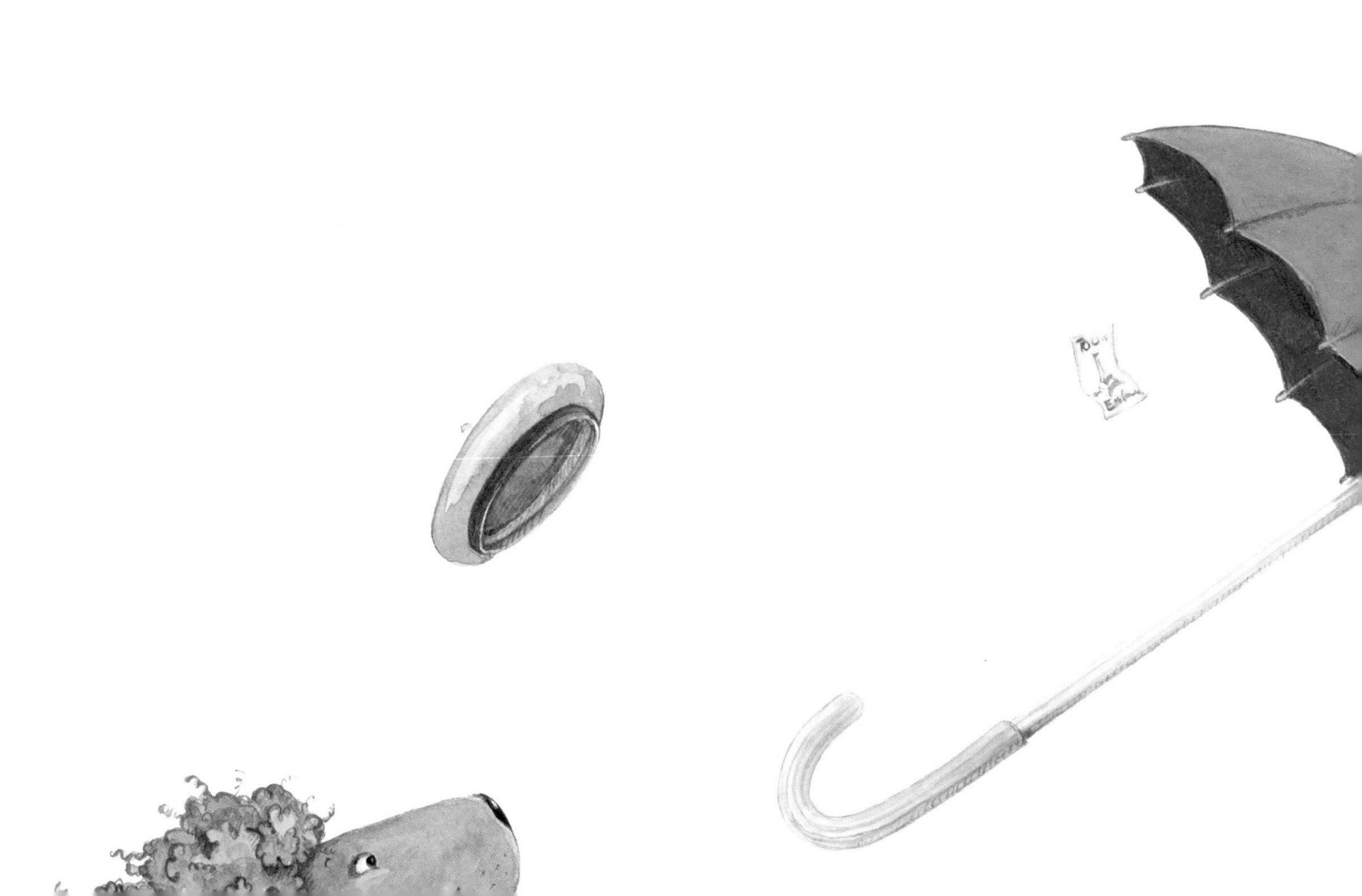

To Kevin,
who can fly over Paris

Library and Archives Canada Cataloguing in Publication

Beck, Andrea, 1956-
Pierre in the air! / Andrea Beck.

Issued also in electronic format.
ISBN 978-1-55469-032-9

I. Title.
PS8553.E2948P39 2011   JC813'.54   C2011-903469-7

Summary: Pierre is in Paris for a dog show and sets out on an adventure that takes him all the way to the top of the Eiffel Tower.

First published in the United States, 2011
Library of Congress Control Number: 2011929238

Orca Book Publishers is dedicated to preserving the environment and has printed this book on paper certified by the Forest Stewardship Council®.

Orca Book Publishers gratefully acknowledges the support for its publishing programs provided by the following agencies: the Government of Canada through the Canada Book Fund and the Canada Council for the Arts, and the Province of British Columbia through the BC Arts Council and the Book Publishing Tax Credit.

Cover and interior artwork created using watercolour and pencil crayon.

Cover and interior artwork by Andrea Beck
Design by Teresa Bubela

ORCA BOOK PUBLISHERS
PO BOX 5626, STN. B
VICTORIA, BC CANADA
V8R 6S4

ORCA BOOK PUBLISHERS
PO BOX 468
CUSTER, WA USA
98240-0468

www.orcabook.com
Printed and bound in Canada.

14 13 12 11 • 4 3 2 1

Pierre in the Air!

ANDREA BECK

ORCA BOOK PUBLISHERS

Pierre Le Poof gobbled down his breakfast, dashed to the living room and jumped up to his seat in the big bay window. He found a comfy spot amongst his toys, bones and Miss Murphy's magazines. Then Pierre gazed out at the world and dreamed of adventure!

“Come, Pierre,” called Miss Murphy. “Your pompoms need a trim for the poodle show.”

Adventurers don’t have pompoms, thought Pierre.

At Poochelli’s Pet Parlor, he wiggled and squirmed until he heard Miss Murphy say the poodle show was in Paris.

Pierre’s ears pricked up.

Paris? He had seen the Eiffel Tower on TV. French Brie was his favorite cheese!

Oooo la la, thought Pierre. This could mean adventure!

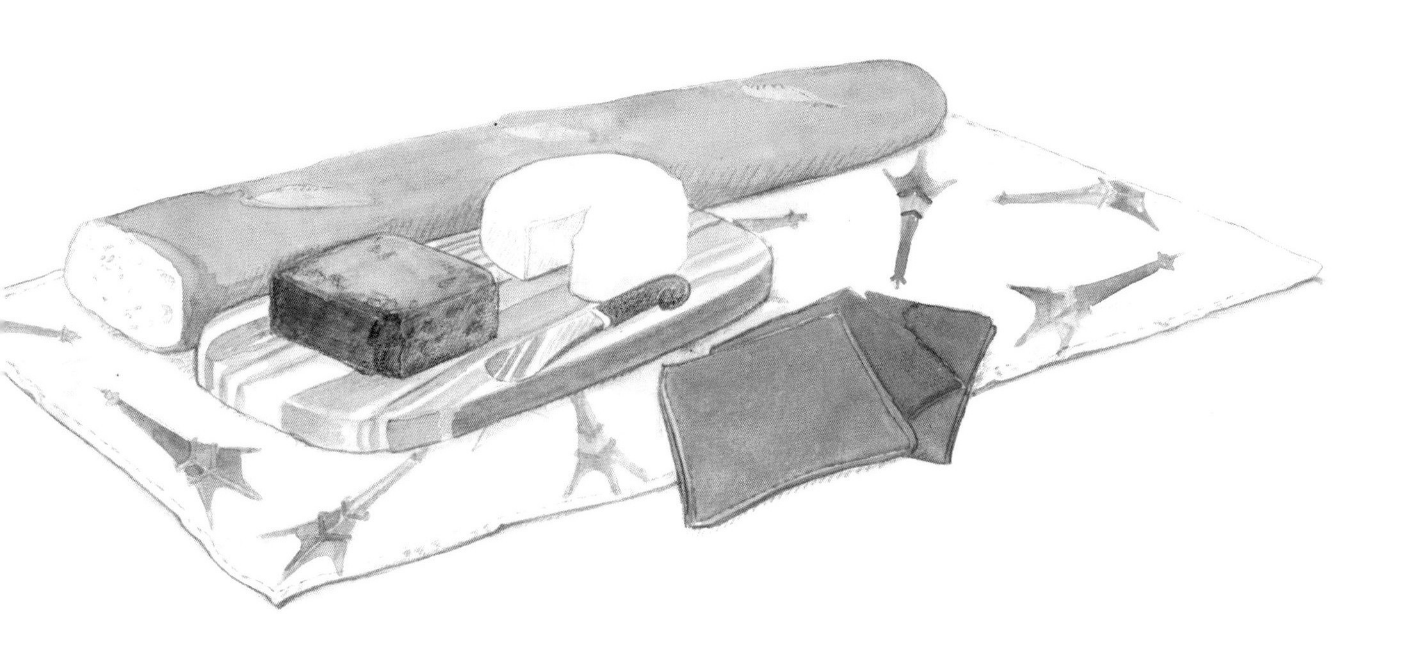

Pierre forgot about pompoms.

He imagined French bread, duck pâté and climbing the Eiffel Tower. While he dreamed, the scissors snipped, and soon he was perfectly poofy once again.

TAXI

The very next day, Pierre and Miss Murphy flew to Paris. On the way to their hotel, Pierre spotted the Eiffel Tower. "Arrooooo!" he howled. His adventure had begun.

After a short nap and a delicious brunch, Pierre was ready to explore the city. When Miss Murphy picked up her purse, he found his leash and scampered to the door.

"I'm sorry, Pierre, they don't allow dogs on the tour," said Miss Murphy.

Then she left without him!

Pierre stalked out to the balcony.

This was not fair! Miss Murphy usually took him everywhere. He could smell bakeries and cafés. He could hear dogs barking and people chatting. In the distance, the tip of the Eiffel Tower beckoned.

Tomorrow she will take me with her, thought Pierre.

The following day, Miss Murphy left Pierre behind again.

He paced. He scratched. He chewed.

Then he sat on the balcony and dreamed he was Pierre Le Poof—Daredevil Poodle. He scaled the Eiffel Tower in record time and parachuted down—and he didn't have pompoms.

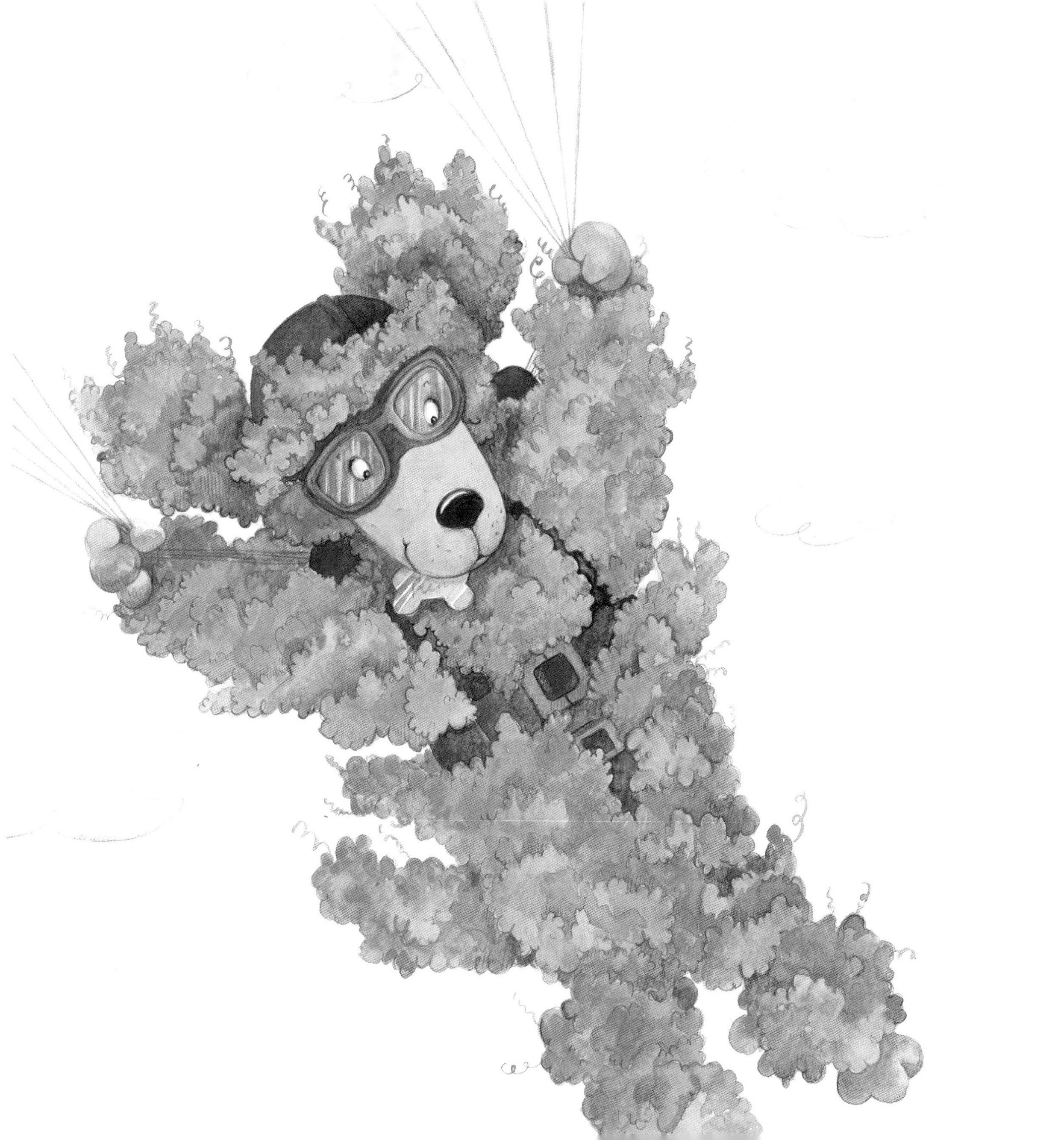

Hotel
Chez
Paris

On their third day in Paris, Miss Murphy said, "I'm sorry to leave you again, Pierre. Today is my only chance to visit the Louvre Museum. The poodle show is tonight, and tomorrow we leave."

Enough is enough! thought Pierre.

The moment the door closed, he slipped under the balcony railing, slid down an awning and leapt to the street below.

With or without Miss Murphy, he was going to climb the Eiffel Tower.

A dog named Coco offered to show Pierre the sights. On their way to the tower, she pointed out the alley with the smelliest Dumpster and the street with the stinkiest cheese shop. Pierre wagged his tail nonstop.

When they arrived at the Eiffel Tower, Pierre snuck past the guard and charged up the stairs. “Arrooooo!” he howled at the top.

Arrooooo
ATTENTION ATTENTION ATTENTION
Fermé
Closed

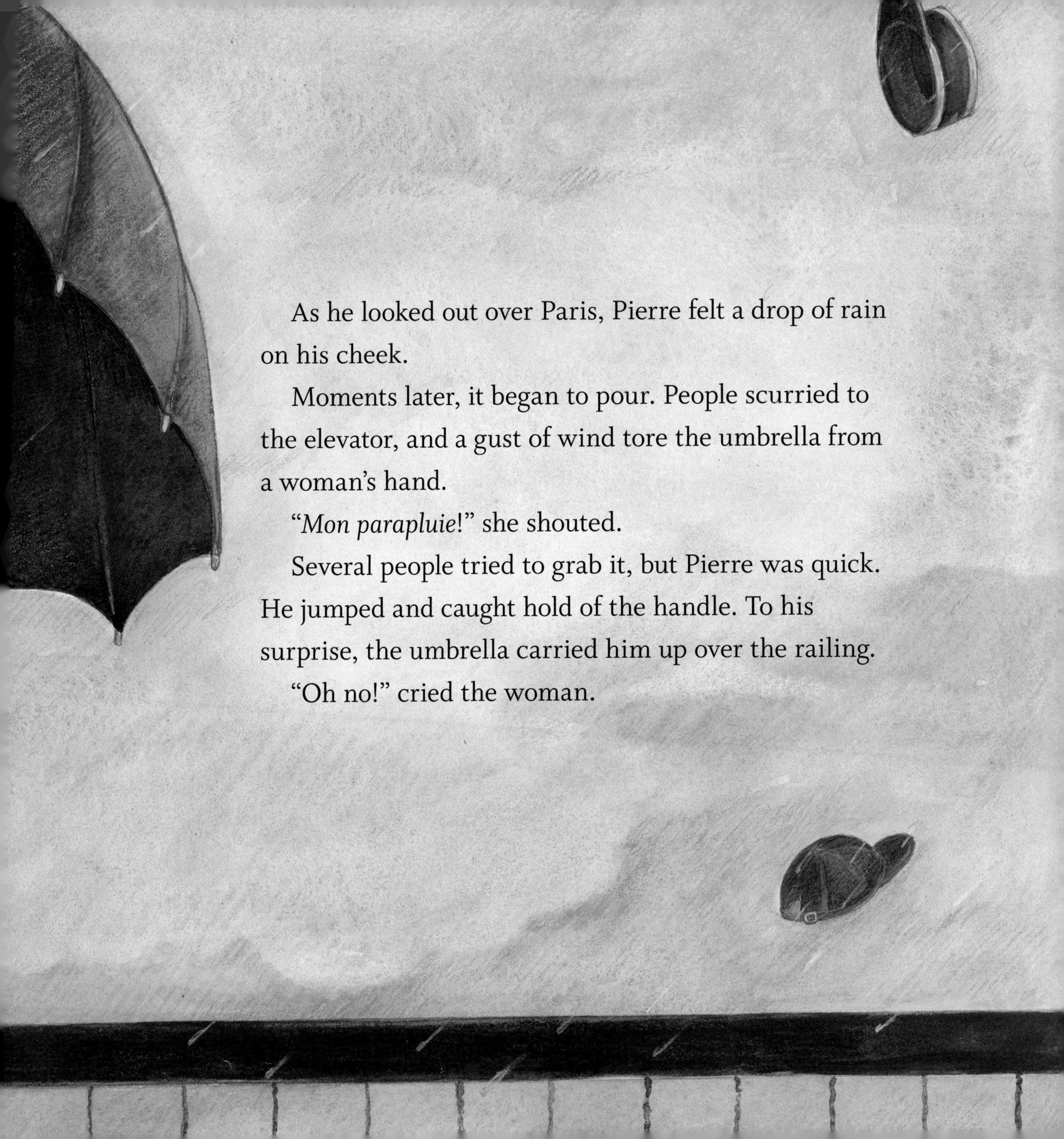

As he looked out over Paris, Pierre felt a drop of rain on his cheek.

Moments later, it began to pour. People scurried to the elevator, and a gust of wind tore the umbrella from a woman's hand.

"*Mon parapluie*!" she shouted.

Several people tried to grab it, but Pierre was quick. He jumped and caught hold of the handle. To his surprise, the umbrella carried him up over the railing.

"Oh no!" cried the woman.

Pierre inched up the handle and held on tight.

"Arrooooo!" he howled joyfully once again.

The storm passed, the clouds cleared and the sun came out.

Pierre drifted to the ground. People cheered, and a photographer snapped his picture.

"Bravo!" said Coco.

After a quick snack at the Dumpster, Pierre ran back to the hotel and scrambled up the awning to the balcony. He shook off the rain and was curling up on the couch when a key turned in the lock.

Pierre sighed happily. Miss Murphy will never know I've been gone, he thought.

Pierre was wrong.

"What have you done?" shrieked Miss Murphy. She snapped the balcony doors shut. "The poodle show is tonight, and you are a mess!"

Before she could say another word, Pierre skedaddled into the tub. Miss Murphy gave him a good scrub. Then she puffed and fluffed him to poofy perfection.

At the show, Pierre walked perfectly, he stood perfectly and he held his head just the right way.

The judge announced his name.

The crowd cheered.

"My champion!" cried Miss Murphy.

I am your champion, thought Pierre, with a wag of his tail. I am also Pierre Le Poof—Daredevil Poodle.

The next morning, Miss Murphy squinted at a photo in the newspaper. It showed a dog sailing through the sky. "What an amazing dog," she said. "He looks a bit like you, Pierre."

"Woof!" said Pierre.

On the way to the airport, Miss Murphy told the driver their next dog show was in Australia.

Pierre sat up straight.

Australia?

He had seen Australia on TV too!

"Arroooooooo-ooo-ooo."